JUNIOR KROLL

BY BETTY PARASKEVAS

ILLUSTRATED BY MICHAEL PARASKEVAS

HARCOURT BRACE JOVANOVICH, PUBLISHERS

SAN DIEGO   NEW YORK   LONDON

Requests for permission to make copies of
any part of the work should be mailed to: Permissions
Department, Harcourt Brace Jovanovich, Publishers,
8th Floor, Orlando, Florida 32887.

Library of Congress Cataloging-in-Publication Data
Paraskevas, Betty.
Junior Kroll/by Betty Paraskevas; illustrated by Michael
Paraskevas. — 1st ed.
p.   cm.
Summary: Humorous poems depict various events in a lively
young boy's life, including taking his baby cousin for a walk,
disrupting a garden club meeting, and making an unusual
birthday cake for his grandfather.
ISBN 0-15-241497-5
1. Children's poetry. American.
[1. American poetry.
2. Humorous poetry.]
I. Paraskevas, Michael, 1961–   ill.
II. Title.
PS3566.A627J86   1993
811'.54 — dc20   92-14207

First edition
A B C D E

The illustrations in this book were done in gouache
on bristol board.
The text type was set in Simoncini Garamond by
Thompson Type, San Diego, California.
The display type was hand-lettered by the illustrator.
Color separations by Bright Arts, Ltd., Singapore
Printed and bound by Tien Wah Press, Singapore
Production supervision by Warren Wallerstein
and Fran Wager
Designed by Michael Farmer

HBJ

Junior Kroll has been a weekly feature in
Dan's Papers, Bridgehampton, New York,
since June 8, 1990.

How fortunate to find people who see what we see;
what a stroke of luck to work with the best —

To Diane D'Andrade and Michael Farmer.

— B. P. and M. P.

THE BIRTHDAY CAKE

Junior Kroll decided to bake
Grandfather Kroll a birthday cake.
He agreed that Mom could supervise,
But the decoration must be a surprise.
So she left the kitchen when the cake was done,
Arming him with an icing gun.
Junior closed the kitchen door
And busied himself for an hour or more.
Green icing, red icing, chocolate, too —
Hurry up, hurry up, so much to do.

Grandfather Kroll closed his eyes.
Junior brought out his big surprise:
The most beautiful cake the family'd ever seen,
Covered with icing, the brightest green.
There were little chocolate spiders and little chocolate flies,
With little red dots for their mean little eyes.
Everyone agreed the cake was enticing,
But everyone managed to scrape off the icing.

THE OLD LADY WHO LIVED DOWN THE LANE

Junior Kroll liked to ride his bike
Down to the end of the lane,
Where the entrance to a huge estate
Was blocked by an iron chain.
Under the chain rode Junior Kroll,
Down the path, and 'round the flagpole.
And every day, weather permitting,
He'd stick out his tongue at the old lady sitting
On the veranda. She'd shake her cane
As Junior raced back down the lane.
Then one day as Junior swung
'Round the flagpole and stuck out his tongue,
He saw an empty rocking chair
And wondered why she wasn't there.
Five days later he rang the bell.
The butler told him she hadn't been well
And directed him to the library, where
The old lady rested in a tapestried chair.
Junior gave her a rose, the most perfect she'd ever seen,
He'd borrowed it, he said, from her neighbor, Mrs. Green.
The old lady laughed for the first time in weeks;
Junior the thief had brought color to her cheeks.

Junior Kroll still rode his bike
Down to the end of the lane,
Where the entrance to a huge estate
Was blocked by an iron chain.
Down the path and around he swung,
Just by the flagpole he'd stick out his tongue.
And the old lady would shake her cane
As Junior raced back down the lane.
Except on Fridays, when Junior would be
On the veranda having biscuits and tea.

CRAZY MAX

Crazy Max, the Krolls' Great Dane
Was a time bomb ticking on the end of a chain.
He chewed the drapes, he ate the flowers,
He dug up the lawn, he barked for hours.
They packed his shoe and sent him away
To Fido U. He was back the next day
With a note that read, "Beyond Control."
He'd only answer to Junior Kroll.
Every day Junior walked Max to town.
When they got to the bakery Max sat down;
He wouldn't budge, he'd sit and wait
For his jelly donut on a paper plate.
Yet, as bad as he was, the Krolls' Great Dane
Loved the little boy on the end of his chain.

THE GARDEN CLUB

Junior Kroll sat among
The Garden Club ladies,
Stretching his tongue,
Trying to touch the tip of his nose,
While someone lectured
On the joy of the rose.
Junior was waiting
For the Key Lime Pie,
But his chair tipped over
As the maid walked by.
He tripped the maid,
She flipped the pie,
And the guests got served
In the blink of an eye.
Crazy Max rushed in
And lapped up the floor,
Plus several guests
As they rushed out the door.
Now Mother has a headache,
The maid has a cane,
Crazy Max is in the basement
Barking on a chain.
Junior's in trouble,
Banished to his room;
But in spite of it all,
The roses still bloom.

THE TANGERINE BEAR

Junior Kroll's bear sat in a chair.
He never went out, but he didn't care.
His fur was worn, and there were spots
Where the cloth showed through, and lots
Of sun had turned him the color of tangerine.
His paws were mended with brown velveteen.
Rides in the stroller, trips to the store,
A day at the beach, a walk on the shore —
Those days were gone. He stayed in his chair
Until it was dark, then he'd fly through the air,
Pulled by one paw, and be tucked into bed.
But that was after Mrs. Kroll said,
"Sleep tight, dear Junior," and turned off the light.

Then the tangerine bear kissed Junior good night.

MORE ABOUT THE TANGERINE BEAR

Junior Kroll's cousin came to stay
At Junior's house while Aunt Jane was away.
Honey Duff brought all her stuff,
But as much as she brought it wasn't enough.
As soon as she saw the tangerine bear
She pulled him out of his little chair.
With the wisdom of mothers, Mrs. Kroll said no,
But Honey Duff screamed and wouldn't let go.
Junior looked up from his picture book
And said *he* didn't mind if Honey Duff took
That dumb old bear, he couldn't care less.
So Honey got the bear and no one would guess
How sad Junior felt when he climbed into bed
And saw the empty chair. Though he never said
A word, when Mrs. Kroll turned off his light
She noticed Junior's eyes were shut awfully tight.

Four days later Honey Duff
Went back home with all her stuff.
She kissed her cousin, Junior Kroll,
And gave back the bear, bless her soul.
Later that night the tangerine bear
Found himself flying through the air,
Pulled by one paw, and tucked into bed.
"Good night, dumb old bear," Junior Kroll said.

THE BABYSITTER

Junior Kroll asked Aunt Jane
If he could take Baby for a stroll down the lane.
Now she's strapped in her buggy, READY, SET, GO.
Aunt Jane is watching, better start nice and slow.
Down the driveway, turn right on the lane,
Hitting each puddle left by the rain.
Baby is laughing, there's mud on her dress,
Faster and faster goes the Kroll Express . . .
Oops! Something's wrong, caught in a hole.
Baby is sinking, it's Junior Kroll
To the rescue, push real hard.
Now let's take a shortcut through Mrs. Green's yard.
Right through the garden, see the flowers in bloom.
Why is the gardener shaking his broom?
Rolling along on wobbly wheels,
Off we go through the strawberry fields.

One shoe is gone. But baby wants more.
Turn down Main Street to the ice cream store.

Back at the house poor Aunt Jane
Looks up and down the driveway, up and down the lane.
Where can they be? She gets in the car.
The Main Street sweet shop! There they are.
In the broken-down buggy, Baby's a mess.
Junior's wiping her hands with the hem of her dress.
Junior's in trouble. Mom and Aunt Jane
Are waiting for Dad so Junior can explain.
Baby's asleep, dreaming of her stroll.
She'll always love her cousin, Junior Kroll.

THE CHICKEN POT PIE

Junior Kroll looked so cute
In his brand-new, navy blue, double-breasted suit,
With shiny brass buttons and a tiny bow tie.
Mother said, "Junior, hold the chicken pot pie.
I forgot to close the windows and it looks like rain.
I'll only be a minute, then we'll visit Aunt Jane."
Junior was uneasy, his arms began to ache.
But if he put the pie down on the ground, the dish might break.
If only Mom would hurry! His eyes were playing tricks:
The pie was getting bigger; his arms were wooden sticks.
The telephone rang. This could be a disaster.
She always talked too long, and the pie was growing faster.
And then a bumble bee came circling 'round and 'round.
Junior simply had no choice: he put the pie down on the ground.

That bee decided to land on Junior's nose.
Junior Kroll stepped back on the nozzle of the hose.
The hose went wild with a powerful spray.
As hard as Junior tried, he couldn't get away.
Then he slipped on the grass and felt his feet fly;
He made a perfect landing in the chicken pot pie.
That's where Mother found him. She turned off the hose
And dragged him in the house to change his brand-new clothes.

Poor Junior Kroll, stuffed in last year's pants,
On his way to see Aunt Jane. He never had a chance
To tell Mother how he wound up in the chicken pot pie.
She wouldn't even listen. Well, he wasn't going to cry.

A VISIT TO THE KINGDOM OF CARDS

Junior Kroll went to stay
At Grandfather's house
While his folks were away.
And every evening Grandfather played
A game of cards with Ruby, the maid.
So it came to pass that Junior Kroll
Learned the skill of self-control,
And the art of playing close to the vest
In the game of poker. And he learned from the best.
Before he went home his grandfather said,
"In the kingdom of cards you keep your head.
You're on your own, there's no one to blame.
If you tip your hand, you lose the game.
And always play a gentleman's hand."
Junior didn't really understand,
But he always remembered those evenings he played
Poker with Grandfather and Ruby, the maid.

LOBSTER

Junior heard Mom say there'd be lobster on the menu,
But he paid no attention till she said, "I'm going to send you
To pick up the lobsters. They'll be in a sack,
Take your wagon to carry them back."
On the way home he was most surprised
When he saw the sack move and realized
The lobsters were alive. He asked Mrs. Kroll,
Busy beating eggs with a whisk in a bowl,
Why the fish market didn't do the deed.
She answered, nonchalantly, there was no need.
All you had to do was get the water boiling hot,
Then drop the lobsters, one by one, into the pot.
Junior was shocked beyond belief.
This was the woman whose chief
Concern was saving whales,
With fancy luncheons and dumb cake sales.
He had to do something, so he went to his dad.
And his reaction was just as bad.
He agreed with Mom, that's how it was done.
Drop them in alive, one by one.
Junior thought it over and took it on himself
To remove the sack from the refrigerator shelf.
He put the lobsters in his wagon, took them to the sea,
Removed their handcuffs, and set them free.

The china sparkled, the silver shined,
The guests grew hungry, but the maid couldn't find
A single lobster to drop in the pot
That held the water, boiling hot.
A nervous Mrs. Kroll announced the delay,
But the take-out shop is on their way
With baby back ribs and super French fries;
Junior's in the leather chair trying to cross his eyes.

THE THANKSGIVING DAY GUEST

Junior Kroll opened the door
For his mother's great-aunt Flo.
She always came the day before,
The day after Thanksgiving she'd go.
She always wore the same black coat
With King Kong for a collar,
And she always gave Junior a Christmas card
On Thanksgiving Day with a dollar.
Junior didn't like her.
She had a funny smell:
Lavender and moth balls.
She made everybody yell.
She insisted on making the stuffing
And Mom never said a word.
But who ever heard of oysters
In the Thanksgiving bird?
She decided on Thanksgiving morning
She'd like to go for a walk.
Mom ordered Junior to tag along.
And soon they started to talk.
She told him of traveling to Istanbul
On the Orient Express,
Long ago when women reporters
Were rare with United Press.
The next morning her cab was waiting
Under a cold gray sky.
From the doorway Mrs. Kroll watched Junior kiss
A remarkable old lady good-bye.

AT THE MOVIES

Junior Kroll went to a matinee,
"For kids only" on a rainy day.
Before the show started he changed his seat
Fifteen times. Then he went for a treat.
Back up the aisle, end of the line.
What'll it be? Popcorn sounds fine.
Wait for the change, "Hey, I gave you a ten."
The picture has started! Down the aisle again.
Can't find the seat, "Excuse me, please,
That's my raincoat. Move your knees."
"I'm telling the usher. He took my seat."
"He's got my raincoat under his feet."
"Well, excuse me, please, it's not MY fault."
This popcorn just has too much salt,
Back up the aisle, check the snack bar sign.
"Hey, kid, get to the end of the line."
Squeeze ahead. "Don't push me."
"Okay, sonny, what'll it be?"
One lemonade, jumbo size,
Some Mexican Hats and licorice bow ties,
One Good & Plenty, some gummy bears, too,
Chocolate kisses, and one large nut chew,
Two bags of lemon drops, to last through the show.
One bag to eat and one bag to throw.

READY TO GO

Junior Kroll is ready to go.
Hooray, hooray! It's the very first snow.
First he's gotta find something to wear:
Warm socks, make that two pair.
T-shirt, Mickey Mouse sweater,
It's really cold, two'll be better.
Now the closet, open the door.
Shoes, slippers, sneakers, flippers
Go flying across the floor.
Boots, boots, where can they be?
No use getting panicky.
Here they are! Gee, they're tight!
Got 'em on backwards, now they're right.
Here's the jacket. Tough getting in.
Zip the zipper up to the chin.
Hat, scarf, and *here we go!*
Gotta make a man out of that snow.
There's the mirror, cast a glance!
Poor Junior Kroll forgot his pants.

THE SWING QUARTET

Junior Kroll tried the saxophone,
The drums and piano, too.
But he found instant gratification
In a ninety-eight-cent kazoo.
All through the day, Junior Kroll
Kazooed along with Billy Joel.
And he brought his kazoo when he went to stay
At Grandfather's house while his folks were away.
Grandfather Kroll and Ruby, the maid,
Were impressed by the way that Junior played.
Grandfather went out and bought two more kazoos,
And he and Ruby taught Junior the blues.
They tackled Benny Goodman's "Sing, Sing, Sing,"
Lordy, that trio could really swing.
When the Krolls returned, Dad said with a grin,
If they didn't mind, he'd like to sit in.
He auditioned well and you can bet
That trio became the Swing Quartet.
When Grandfather Kroll had a Christmas party,
They entertained the guests;
The Swing Quartet was such a hit
They began to get requests:
"One O'Clock Jump," "Sleepy Lagoon,"
"Song of India," "Fly Me to the Moon."
Then Grandfather gave each guest a kazoo,
And they improvised till after two.

WHAT ARE YOU DOING NEW YEAR'S EVE?

Junior Kroll had a date
With Grandfather Kroll to celebrate
New Year's Eve, home alone,
Just two guys on their own . . .
The radio issued bulletins all day,
Warning that snow was on the way.
So they went into town to get supplies,
And Grandfather said he had a surprise.
At the video store he picked out the best
Of W. C. Fields, then on for the rest
Of the things they'd need: a top hat for Max,
Two paper derbies, some video snacks,
The longest, fanciest horns they could find,
And chocolate cigars for after they'd dined.
They turned on the lights on the Christmas tree,
And the VCR with W. C.
The pizza arrived along with the sleet
That tapped on the windows and danced on the street.
In paper derbies they watched TV,
And they dined with the king of comedy.

Junior Kroll would never forget
That New Year's Eve and the night he met
W. C. Fields. What a memory to keep!
But midnight found them fast asleep.